panda series

**PANDA books are for young readers
making their own way
through books.**

BAINTE DEN STOC

WITHDRAWN FROM
DÚN LAOGHAIRE-RATHDOWN COUNTY
LIBRARY STOCK

KT-371-862

O'BRIEN SERIES FOR YOUNG READERS

 panda cubs

 pandas

 panda legends

flyers

'A charming story ... good text, well illustrated
by the writer's fine line drawings.'

EVENING HERALD

'This charming book recounts the adventure of
an outcast little sheep – how he saved the
whole flock in a snowstorm and gave the
shepherd a bright idea. That put the bossy
sheepdog in its place! Fine line drawings
illustrate this simple and memorable story.'

EVENING PRESS

ELIZABETH SHAW

Elizabeth Shaw was born in Belfast and lived in East Berlin from 1946 until her death in 1992. She was widely known as an author and illustrator of children's books in German. Her work was exhibited in Berlin, London, Munich and Belfast, among other places. She won several prizes, including the Käthe Kollwitz Prize at the Academy of Art, Berlin, the Leipzig Silver Medal, the Hans Baltzer Prize, and the DDR Art Prize.

The Little Black Sheep

Written and illustrated by
• ELIZABETH SHAW •

THE O'BRIEN PRESS
DUBLIN

First published in hardback 1985 by The O'Brien Press Ltd,
12 Terenure Road East, Rathgar, Dublin 6, Ireland.
Reprinted 1989.
First published in paperback 1995.
Published in the Panda series 1997.
Reprinted 1998, 1999, 2000, 2003, 2007, 2012, 2014.

Copyright for text and illustrations © Elizabeth Shaw Estate

ISBN: 978-0-86278-463-8

All rights reserved. No part of this book may be
reproduced or utilised in any form or by any means, electronic
or mechanical, including photocopying, recording or by any
information storage or retrieval system without
permission in writing from the publisher.

11 13 15 16 14 12

14 16 18 17 15

Editing, typesetting, layout and design: The O'Brien Press Ltd
Cover illustration: redrawn and recoloured by Susan Cooper
Illustrations: Elizabeth Shaw
Printed and bound by Clondalkin Digital Print
The paper use in this book is produced using pulp
from managed forests

The O'Brien Press receives financial assistance from

A NOTE ON TRANSLATIONS

The Little Black Sheep
has been translated into German, Swedish,
Danish, Spanish, Portuguese, Latvian,
Turkish and Japanese.
In Japan it was a major bestseller.

Can YOU spot the panda
hidden in the story?

Once there was a shepherd
who lived far away
in the mountains.
He had a sheepdog called Polo,
who helped him
to look after the sheep.

Polo watched the sheep
while the shepherd sat
on a mossy rock and knitted.
He knitted socks and scarves and
pullovers and blankets made of
pure sheep's wool, and sold them
at the village market.

When the shepherd noticed that
a sheep was straying
too far from the flock,
he took out a wooden whistle
and blew a short blast on it.
This was a signal for Polo
to run after the sheep and
chase it back to the others.
Polo felt **very important** then.

At sunset the shepherd blew
a long blast on his whistle
and this meant that Polo
should round up the sheep
and chase them into the fold.
As they jumped over the stile,
the shepherd counted them
to make sure that all were there.

All the sheep were white
except one, the little black sheep.
When Polo barked '**All to
the left**' or '**Right turn!**
or '**Halt**' they all did
what they were told.
All, that is, except the little
black one who often turned
to the left when he should turn
to the right because he was
thinking of something else.
This annoyed Polo.

'That black sheep does not obey me!' Polo complained to the shepherd. 'And he thinks too much! Sheep don't need to think. I think for them!'

The little black sheep wished
he were like the others.
'Polo notices when I make a
mistake because I'm black,'
he said to the shepherd.
'Could you not knit me
a little white jacket
so that I wouldn't be
so noticeable?'

'No indeed,' replied the shepherd,
'you are a very handy little sheep.
When I count you all
jumping into the fold,
I could easily fall asleep.
But I am always jerked awake
by my little black sheep
jumping over the stile,
especially if you stumble.'

Polo, however, liked order and
discipline in the flock.
'You just wait!' he snarled
at the black sheep, 'I'll see
that you are sold after
shearing-time. Then we'll have
a nice tidy flock!'

The little black sheep looked
wistfully at the little white fleecy
clouds in the sky.
'The shepherd says that they are
the souls of good little sheep,'
he thought. 'Maybe one day
I'll be a little white cloud too!'
Then he noticed that
the sky was growing dark
behind the mountain.
'It's going to rain!' he called.
**'I'll tell you when it's
going to rain**' snapped Polo.

A sudden storm broke,
with hail and wind and snow.
'My knitting will be ruined!'
cried the shepherd. 'Come, Polo,
we must run for shelter.'

They ran to the shepherd's
little hut.
'The sheep will be all right.
They have their nice woolly coats.'
He made a cosy fire
to dry his things and
had a drink or two.

Night fell.

'We'll see the sheep tomorrow,'
said the shepherd.

'No need to worry,' said Polo,
'they'll stay where they are
because I'm not there to tell them
what to do,' and he stretched out
beside the fire.

Meanwhile, the sheep were getting
nervous and upset.

'Where is Polo?' they bleated.

'What are we to do?'

'We must look for shelter,'
said the little black sheep.

'Follow me! I think I know
where there's a cave!'

He led them up the hill
to where there were some hollow
rocks with an overhanging ledge.
'We must stay close together
and keep each other warm.
I'll look out for the shepherd
when it's light,' said the
little black sheep.

t morning the snow
had stopped falling, but
as far as the eye could see
all was white.
'Finding sheep today is like
trying to find an ice cream
dropped near the North Pole,'
said the shepherd.

'I am a bad shepherd,'
he sighed, and he wished
he had not drunk so much
the night before. 'Now I've
lost my sheep!'
'And how will they manage
without **me** ?' muttered Polo.

Then they saw a black spot
on the top of the hill.
'Polo!' cried the shepherd,
'perhaps it is our little
black sheep!'
They hurried towards it.

Under the ledge of rock
they found all the sheep.
There was great rejoicing.
'My little black sheep!'
said the shepherd fondly,
'but for you I might not have
found my flock.'
'Well, maybe he is useful as a
landmark, if nothing else,'
growled Polo jealously.

The sun came out and
the snow melted.

**'Form ranks! Forward
march!'** barked Polo.

The shepherd carried the
little black sheep down
the hill himself.

'I always said you were
a handy little sheep,' he said.

When shearing-time came,
the shepherd put the wool
into sacks. There were
ten sacks of white wool and
one little sack of black wool.
'Now, how about selling
that black sheep?' suggested Polo.
'Then we would have
a tidy, orderly flock.'
'No indeed!' replied the shepherd,
'I have an idea!'

'I can knit lovely patterns
out of black and white wool!'
He knitted patterned socks
and scarves and blankets,
and sold them for a good price
at the market.
With the money he bought
some more black sheep.

Soon he had a flock of black,
and white, and spotted sheep.
Each one was different,
and that was nice,
because now they were
all the same.

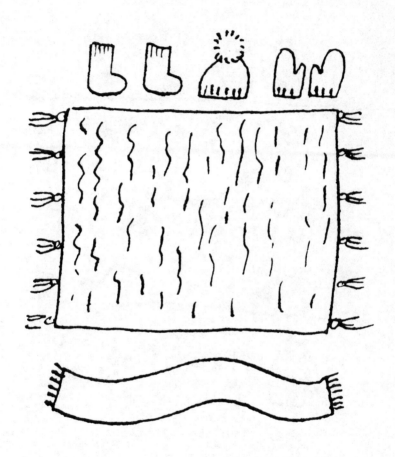

Well, did you find him?